Dog Can Hide

written by **LAURA GEHL**   illustrated by **FRED BLUNT**

Ready-to-Read

Simon Spotlight
New York   London   Toronto   Sydney   New Delhi

Here is a list of all the words you will find in this book. Sound them out before you begin reading the story.

Names:

Cat   Dog   Frog

SIMON SPOTLIGHT

An imprint of Simon & Schuster Children's Publishing Division
1230 Avenue of the Americas, New York, New York 10020
This Simon Spotlight edition January 2023
Text copyright © 2023 by Laura Gehl
Illustrations copyright © 2023 by Fred Blunt
For information about special discounts for bulk purchases, please contact Simon & Schuster
Special Sales at 1-866-506-1949 or business@simonandschuster.com.
Manufactured in the United States of America 1222 LAK
2 4 6 8 10 9 7 5 3 1
Library of Congress Cataloging-in-Publication Data
Names: Gehl, Laura, author. | Blunt, Fred, illustrator. Title: Dog can hide / by Laura Gehl ;
illustrated by Fred Blunt. Description: Simon Spotlight edition. | New York : Simon Spotlight,
2022. | Series: Ready-to-read. Ready to go! | Audience: Ages 3–5 | Summary: Illustrations
and simple text relate how Dog and Frog and Cat play hide and seek. Identifiers: LCCN
2022012202 (print) | LCCN 2022012203 (ebook) | ISBN 9781534499553 (paperback) |
ISBN 9781534499560 (hardcover) | ISBN 9781534499577 (ebook) Subjects: CYAC: Stories
in rhyme. | Hide-and-seek—Fiction. Classification: LCC PZ8.3.G273 Dg 2022 (print)
LCC PZ8.3.G273 (ebook) | DDC [E]—dc23
LC record available at https://lccn.loc.gov/2022012202
LC ebook record available at https://lccn.loc.gov/2022012203

Word families:

"-at" → cat   hat   mat

"-eek" → creek   eek   peek   seek

"-og" → bog   dog   frog   log

"-urp" → burp   slurp

Sight words:

a   and   by   can   find

fly   in   is   not   the

Bonus words:

| buzz | cannot | hide |

Ready to go? Happy reading!

Don't miss the questions about the story
on the last page of this book.

Dog can hide.
Frog can hide.

Cat can seek.

Frog can hide
in a log.

Cat cannot peek.

Dog can hide
in a mat.

Cat cannot peek.

Cat can seek.

Cat can seek
by the bog.

BUZZ! BUZZ!
Frog can find a fly.

SLURP!

BURP!

Cat can find Frog!

Cat and Frog seek.

Cat and Frog
seek by the creek.

EEK!!!

Dog is not
by the creek.

Cat and Frog find the mat.

Cat and Frog
find Dog!

Cat can hide.
Frog can hide.

Dog can seek.

Dog can seek
by the hat.

Dog can find Cat!

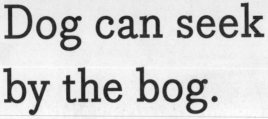

Dog can seek
by the bog.

Dog cannot
find Frog.

Dog can seek
by the creek.

Dog cannot
find Frog.

Dog can find Frog!

Now that you have read the story, can you answer these questions?

1. At the beginning of the story, who is seeking? Who is seeking at the end of the story?

2. How does Dog trick Frog into coming out of his hiding spot?

3. In this story you read the words "cat" and "hat" and "mat." Those words rhyme! Can you think of other words that rhyme with "cat" and "hat" and "mat"?

Great job!
You are a reading star!